The
Gathering Tree

The
Gathering Tree

Larry Loyie

with Constance Brissenden

Illustrated by Heather D. Holmlund

Library and Archives Canada Cataloguing in Publication

Loyie, Larry, 1933-
The gathering tree / Larry Loyie with Constance Brissenden

Includes bibliographical references.
ISBN 1-894778-28-6

1. HIV infections--Juvenile fiction. 2. AIDS (Disease)--Juvenile
fiction.
3. Indians of North America--Juvenile fiction. I. Brissenden, Constance, 1947-

II. Title.

PS8573.O979G38 2005   jC813'.6   C2005-904628-7

Printed in Canada

Printed on Ancient Forest Friendly 100% post consumer fibre paper.

www.theytus.com
In Canada:
Theytus Books, Green Mountain Rd.,
Lot 45, RR#2, Site 50, Comp. 8
Penticton, BC, V2A 6J7, Tel: 250-493-7181
In the USA:
Theytus Books, P.O. Box 2890, Oroville, Washington, 98844

Theytus Books acknowledges the support of the following: We acknowledge the financial support of the Government of Canada through the Canada Book Fund for our publishing activities. We acknowledge the support of the Canada Council for the Arts which last year invested $20.1 million in writing and publishing throughout Canada. Nous remercions de son soutien le Conseil des Arts du Canada, qui a investi 20,1 millions de dollars l'an dernier dans les lettres et l'édition à travers le Canada. We acknowledge the support of the Province of British Columbia through the British Columbia Arts Council.

This book was initiated, supported and guided by Chee Mamuk, Aboriginal Program, STD/AIDS Control, British Columbia Centre for Disease Control. Chee Mamuk and the BC Centre for Disease Control are an agency of the Provincial Health Services Authority which has provided additional funding.

Dedications

To all Aboriginal people with HIV/AIDS and what we learn from them.

In memory of William (Bill) Hugh Walkem and Tyler Don Mountain Twin, who inspired the characters of Bill and Tyler.

The boy ran along the old trail with ease. His moccasins made little noise. The wind was cool on his face and the forest was quiet. He watched for animals like his grandfather had taught him. He thought he glimpsed a deer on a distant hill.

A few more hills and I'll reach the village, he thought. The people will be happy to hear the news I'm bringing. Soon everyone will know about the gathering at the old tree this weekend.

Coming into the clearing, he saw his home. His sister Shay-Lyn and her best friend Kelly were playing soccer in the yard.

The pictures in his mind faded. Once again he was Tyler, and not a messenger running in times long ago. Thinking of the old stories made him run better. As he stretched his sore muscles after his run, Tyler felt good inside.

Shay-Lyn kicked the ball in front of her, using the side of her foot. Her eyes were on the red ribbon dangling from the clothesline. She kicked hard. Tyler watched the soccer ball sail toward the target and hit it.

"She scores!," Tyler yelled. His voice echoed against the rolling hills behind their house.

Tyler was proud of Shay-Lyn. His sister was a good soccer player already and practised hard. His dream was to be a great runner one day, like his cousin Robert who ran marathons. Most of all, he wanted to be strong like his Dad who was a logger.

From the kitchen window, Dad called to them. "It's getting dark. Time to come in."

Shay-Lyn picked up her soccer ball and waved to Kelly. "See you tomorrow," she said.

Kelly frowned. "I can't come over tomorrow."

"Why not?" Shay-Lyn stared at her.

"Your cousin is coming to stay with you. Mom says he's sick. She doesn't want me visiting."

Kelly jumped on her bike and peddled off.

Shay-Lyn looked at her brother. "What does Kelly mean?" she asked Tyler. Her older brother usually had the answers to confusing questions.

Tyler just shook his head. "I don't know," he said.

The truth was, he didn't understand at all. Sick meant staying in bed. But Robert was not in bed. He was coming to their place tomorrow on the bus.

Mom sat on the floor of the living room, humming a tune. A bright red cloth was spread in front of her. A cutout of a wolf lay nearby.

Shay-Lyn hurried over. "You're making my shawl for the gathering," she said happily.

Mom looked up and smiled. "My grandma taught me many things about our culture and traditions. She told me that wolves are very smart. You work hard in school. I think it's fitting you have a wolf on the back of your shawl."

Dad was at the dining room table, working on a deer hide. Tyler sat down beside him.

"There's just enough deer hide to make you a vest," Dad explained. "We will make it without a needle and thread. I'll make holes with my knife. Then you can pull strips of hide through the holes."

Dad put his hand on Tyler's shoulder. "Is something bothering you? You seem quiet tonight," he said.

Tyler hesitated. Finally he said, "Is Robert really sick?"

Dad put down the vest. He spoke gently. "Why are you asking?"

Shay-Lyn got up from the floor and came close.

"Because Kelly's mom said so." Shay-Lyn's voice shook when she spoke.

Dad's voice was quiet. "We don't want to believe it but it's true. The doctor told Robert that he has HIV. It's a virus that makes people very sick."

Tyler's stomach churned. "Will he get better soon?" he asked.

"Right now there is no cure," Dad said. "The elders asked us to invite Robert to the gathering. They want him to talk to our community to teach us about HIV."

Mom's face was sad. "We'll all be learning together. People don't want to talk about it. And it's already here in our community," she said.

The last time Tyler saw his cousin, Robert was strong and healthy. He won every race he entered. His picture was in the newspaper holding a shining trophy.

Shay-Lyn looked at Tyler. They wanted to know more about Robert's illness but didn't know what to ask. Would their cousin look different now? Could he still run?

They arrived at the depot a few minutes before the bus pulled in. Tyler and Shay-Lyn stood close together.

"I'm scared to see Robert," Shay-Lyn whispered.

Tyler didn't answer. Robert was their favorite cousin. When they were little, he took them everywhere. For a special treat, he even took them to see the wild animals at the zoo.

Dad glanced their way. "Smile, you two," he said. "Your cousin will be here soon."

Mom hugged Shay-Lyn. "Don't worry. You can't catch HIV like you can catch a cold or the flu."

The bus pulled in. Robert was the first to get off.

The children couldn't believe what they saw. Their cousin didn't look sick at all. He wore a cowboy hat and carried his packsack. He had a big smile for them.

"Boy, am I happy to see you folks," he said to Tyler and Shay-Lyn. He hugged the whole family.

Dad took two bicycles off his truck. "The kids are going to bike home," he told Robert.

"I'll run with them. I haven't had my run today." Robert took off his jacket and did some stretches. Tyler and Shay-Lyn stretched with him.

"Maybe I can't beat you but I'm sure going to try," Robert said.

His long legs kicked up the gravel as he raced ahead. Tyler and Shay-Lyn had to peddle hard to keep up.

Their people had used the fishing spots on the river longer than anyone remembered.

Tyler led the way down the hill. A wide ledge overlooked the tumbling river.

Three elders sat near the racks used for drying fish. Bill, the oldest, stood up when he saw the family. Ed and Mary rose to greet them as well. They shook hands with Robert, Mom and Dad.

A helper brought a wooden bowl filled with burning sage. One by one, the family cleansed with the sage. Then they sat down with the elders.

Tyler and Shay-Lyn walked to the rocky ledge. They sat near the edge and peered into the water, watching for salmon swimming up the river.

"How long will Robert be sick?" Shay-Lyn asked after a while.

"You heard what Dad said. There is no cure."

"Kelly says we can get sick if we use the same cup as Robert."

Tyler jumped up. "Kelly doesn't know anything," he said in an angry voice. "Mom told me you couldn't get it that way. You can't get it from being in the same room, or hugging, or sitting on the same toilet."

At the sound of Tyler's voice, Bill walked over to the river. He called to Dad.

"I think it's time you showed your boy how to fish in our traditional way. We still have plenty of daylight left," Bill said.

Dad chose the lightest pole. He held up a special salmon hook and showed Tyler how to attach it to the pole. "Make sure your hook is underwater. The fish will think it's a willow sticking in the water. When you see a salmon, ease the pole toward it as close as you can. Then plunge the pole down hard," he told him.

Dad tied a rope around Tyler's waist, and then tied the rope to a tree. "Now all you have to do is wait for a fish."

Bill stood by, watching as Tyler stepped on to the ledge. "You have to be patient. The fish isn't in a hurry to get caught. It's not going to jump on to your hook," Bill laughed.

Standing on the ledge high above the river, Tyler held the pole in the water. At first it was light, then slowly it began to get heavier. Looking down into the back eddy made Tyler dizzy. He was glad that the feeling passed quickly.

A fish suddenly appeared, swimming slowly toward him. Tyler's heart was beating hard. He eased his pole near the salmon. Now, he thought. With all his strength, he plunged the pole. The salmon was strong and fought hard. Tyler needed his father's help to pull the fish out of the river.

Shay-Lyn ran to Mom. "Tyler's got one," she yelled. Everyone hurried over.

Ed was the first to speak. "We have reason to celebrate. Salmon is the food of life for our people. Tyler is now a provider for his family."

A lone eagle circled high above them, free on the wind.

"Look up, Tyler," Mary said. "The eagle knows you have done well. This day is yours to remember."

"I've caught my first fish," Tyler thought for the hundredth time. He had dreamed of this moment for a long time. He knew if he practised he would be a good fisher one day.

Mom cooked a special meal in his honor. As he ate his salmon, Tyler thought it tasted better than any other.

The sky was a brilliant red from the setting sun. Robert and the elders talked around the fire.

"Let's stop for a special ceremony," Bill said. He called Tyler over. "We will burn some cedar for what you did today."

Tyler stood between his Dad and Robert. Each put a hand on his shoulder.

The small circle stood quietly, watching as the dried cedar burned brightly in the fire.

Everyone watched as Bill put the dried cedar in the bowl and lit it. They were quiet as he prayed softly in their language.

After the prayers, they sat again in the circle.

Bill's eyes were often laughing as he told stories and legends. Now his eyes were serious.

"Long ago we helped our people who got sick," Bill said. "I prayed for support and understanding from our community."

Shay-Lyn moved closer to Mom.

"Are you thinking of Kelly?" Mom whispered. "It must be lonely without your best friend." Shay-Lyn nodded.

Bill turned to Robert. "We would like to hear from you now," he said.

Tyler looked up from the fire. His cousin sat silently for a time. Then Robert looked at each of them in turn.

"I'm only 21," Robert said. For a moment, Tyler thought his cousin was going to cry.

Robert pulled his shoulders back. "The virus is in my body now and I can't get it out. Every day I'm scared of what is going to happen to me. No matter what, I'm going to fight as hard as I can. If I fight long enough, maybe the doctors will find a cure."

No one spoke. The only sound was the rushing of the river.

"All I can do now is speak out about this illness. I'm going to keep on speaking until all of our people hear me. I'm going to tell them they don't have to get this," he said.

Mary came over to Tyler and Shay-Lyn. She gave each of them a handful of loose tobacco.

"Our people burn tobacco as an offering," Mary said. "Burn it in the fire to guide young people and keep them healthy and safe."

Tyler and his sister dropped the tobacco into the fire. Smoke rose into the night.

Robert parked Mom's car in the parking lot. Tyler and Shay-Lyn jumped out and followed their cousin to the entrance of the zoo. Robert bought their tickets and they went inside.

As they walked around the zoo, Shay-Lyn asked, "What animal do you want to be?"

Tyler laughed. "That's easy. I want to be a giraffe. You know I love cherries. If I had a long neck I could pick them all day without a ladder."

They turned a bend and stopped by the wolf pen. They watched three wolves playing together inside.

"I want to be a wolf," Shay-Lyn said. "Wolf parents take good care of their pups. All the other wolves watch over them too."

Finally they came to the tiger's cage. Inside the tiger paced back and forth. His fierce eyes sent a shiver through Tyler.

"I brought you here because I wanted you to see this tiger again," Robert said. "I never liked to see him locked up in a cage. Now I'm just like this tiger."

"You're not in a cage," Shay-Lyn said with a frown.

Robert looked at them sadly. "Now that I have this illness, I can only stay away from the city so long. My doctors are in the city. I need to be near them. That's why I'm like this tiger. We both want to be free but we're not."

"You'll still visit us, won't you?" Tyler asked.

"I'll always come back to see you two," Robert promised. "Now let's go and get some ice cream."

Shay-Lyn twirled around the room, trying out a few dance steps. "Thank you, Mom," she said with a grin. "I love my new shawl."

Tyler's vest fit him perfectly. He liked the way the deer hide fringe hung below his waist.

Mom and Robert sat at the kitchen table finishing breakfast. Robert got up and put the dishes in the sink.

"I'm going up the big hill," Robert said, "to prepare myself, so that I can run over the mountain to the gathering tree."

Mom looked uncertainly at Robert. "Are you sure you're healthy enough to run the marathon?"

"As long as I am able to run, I will," Robert said. "You know, our people have always lived here. Somehow it's like I never really saw our hills before. Now everything I see is beautiful. Being home makes me feel stronger."

Tyler and Shay-Lyn walked with Robert to a lookout high up on the hill.

When they stopped, Robert took four ribbons from his pocket, red, yellow, white and black. Carefully they tied them in the four directions. Then they sat in silence, looking out over the long valley.

"Our gathering place is down there," Robert finally said, pointing to the valley far away. "The old tree is waiting for us. It has waited for our people for generations. The next time I see that tree, I'll be running toward it."

Tyler's words rushed out. "When can I run the marathon? I've been practising hard just like you taught me."

"One day I hope we'll run it together. You'll be a young man then," Robert said.

"Can I run to meet you before you get to the tree?"

"I'll be looking for you," his cousin replied. "We will finish the marathon together."

All day, cars and trucks had arrived in the valley. People came to the gathering from everywhere. Some even brought their horses.

Tents were pitched here and there. Children ran around yelling and playing. Many elders already sat near the dance area. Cedar boughs hung from ropes to mark the speaking area.

Before the sacred fire was lit, helpers cleansed the area with sage and sweetgrass. They would keep the fire going day and night until the gathering was over.

Three white tents were set up. One was for cooking. The second was a resting place for the elders. The third had a sign that read "Health and Wellness Tent."

Nearby, young volunteers dug a salmon pit. Soon fresh salmon would be cooked for the first feast of the gathering.

Tyler stood alone at the gathering tree. Its branches towered over him. The old tree had withstood many storms and gale force winds. Strips of colored cloth were tied around its trunk to honor it.

As he stood beneath the tree, Tyler could feel its power. The old tree's strength surged through his body.

Suddenly he knew it was time. Tyler set out alone, running along the trail. "I'll be the first to welcome Robert," he said to himself.

Tyler heard shouts, and saw Robert running toward him. Young
men and women ran with him. Robert looked tired. Dust and sweat
covered his face.

"Cousin, I was watching for you," Robert said when he saw Tyler.

As Tyler ran beside him, Robert's strides grew stronger. In a few minutes,
they were circling the old tree.

The crowd cheered them on. Tyler tried to look solemn. No matter how
hard he tried he couldn't keep a big grin off his face.

The hand drumming began. The elders were among the first to join the drummers by the old tree. Robert walked with Bill to the speaking area. Shay-Lyn and Tyler moved closer to be near them.

Soon all the people at the gathering made their way to the circle. Tyler saw Kelly and her mom take a seat to listen.

When everyone was settled, Bill stood and looked over the circle. He smiled in his kindly way.

"Welcome, my people," Bill said in his language. "Once again we're here at the gathering tree. This is our healing tree. It stands apart from the other trees for us to come and seek guidance and protection."

He paused and repeated his words in English so that everyone could understand them. Then he continued.

"When I was a boy, my dad taught me how to respect everything that gives us life. It stuck in my head. He said that when the sun and water get together, everything grows. We must thank them every day.

"My grandmother said that our people gathered around anyone who was sick. They brought medicines to heal them. We shared a closeness in those days.

"We lost a good way of life when we were taken to residential school. Slowly, we are getting it back. Our children are learning our languages again. It's a good start.

"We want to keep growing stronger. That is why the elders have invited Robert to speak about HIV. We can't shut out this illness. It's not just in the city but in our own communities as well. We must never be afraid of learning what can help us survive. Let's listen carefully to what Robert has to tell us."

Robert stepped forward. After a moment, he spoke in a quiet voice. "I thought I was Superman when I went to school in the city. I thought I could run through life, winning trophies, partying, and that nothing bad would ever catch up with me."

Robert took a deep breath. "Now I know I'm not Superman."

His voice was stronger now. "At first I didn't tell anyone I had HIV. I backed away from family and friends. I felt scared and lonely. Then I remembered our traditions. If I was going to heal, I had to tell the truth and be open to others.

"After I started speaking out, some of my friends wouldn't talk to me anymore. That's okay. It didn't stop me.

"I want you to know that you don't have to get HIV. It is totally preventable if you learn about it. I'm here to answer any questions you have. I'll be in the health and wellness tent. Don't be afraid to come and see me."

The gathering was quiet as Bill spoke again.

"Come. Let us join Robert in an honor dance," the elder said. "Let us support him in his journey to educate people about this sickness."

The hand drummers were ready. Side by side, Bill and Robert entered the circle.

Tyler turned to his sister. "Let's dance with Robert," he said. They stepped into the circle together. Smiling at Shay-Lyn, Kelly joined them in the circle. Heads held high, the two girls danced their fancy steps.

As he danced, Tyler felt free inside. Just by being family, he knew he was helping Robert be strong. Tyler looked up at the gathering tree standing guard over them. "Thank you for always being here for us," he said silently.

Beside him, Shay-Lyn swung her red shawl in beautiful circles.

To Our Readers

"Why did you write this book?" We are often asked this question.

The answer is simple. We want to make all children aware of HIV, the serious virus that causes AIDS. If a person does not become infected with HIV, they will never get AIDS. More and more children have family members with HIV. We all need to have a better understanding of the illness.

Awareness of this virus can save a person's life.

AWARENESS: having knowledge

HIV/AIDS is a frightening epidemic that has spread quickly around the world. At this time, there is no cure, although there are medicines that can help people with the illness.

Doctors first noticed HIV/AIDS in the early 1980s. Since then, more than 60 million people have been infected. In 2004, the World Health Organization reported that almost 40 million people around the world are living with HIV/AIDS. Almost 5 million new cases were reported in 2004. More than 3 million people died of AIDS that year.

Prevention is the best way to keep these numbers from growing.

PREVENTION: to keep something from happening

HIV/AIDS is totally preventable. Prevention means to stop it before it happens. Many people only become aware of the illness after it has affected someone they know.

Education about HIV/AIDS is important. Individuals, families, communities and countries are suffering because of this illness. Children need to learn how to stay healthy as they grow older. We must all work together to halt the spread of the virus.

SUPPORT: to give strength or help

"Are those real people in your book?"

In *The Gathering Tree*, Tyler, Shay-Lyn, Robert and others seem to be real people. But they are not real people. Only the problems they face in the book are real.

The story takes place in a First Nations setting. It is about a family and a community learning together about a threatening illness. Larry Loyie's love for First Nations cultures and people helped him write with feeling and understanding. Sadly, a story like *The Gathering Tree* could take place anywhere in the world today.

We hope this book encourages children, families and communities to learn more about HIV and AIDS.

More About HIV/AIDS

1. **What is HIV?**

    HIV is the virus that causes AIDS. Only people who have HIV get AIDS.

    HIV stands for Human Immunodeficiency Virus. Deficiency means "not working properly."

    AIDS stands for Acquired Immunodeficiency Syndrome.

2. **What is a virus?**

    A virus is a small germ that gets inside your body and makes more of itself in there. It can make you feel sick. Colds, flu, cold sores and chickenpox are viruses, and so is HIV.

3. **How do people get better from the flu or a cold?**

    Every person's body has an immune system. It is like a set of warriors in the body that fight illnesses, and help you get better. When you have the flu or a cold, the immune system fights off the virus and you get better after awhile.

4. **Can the immune system fight off all viruses?**

    No. HIV attacks the immune system itself and weakens it over time. This makes it hard to fight off infections. Over time HIV leads to AIDS. When a person has AIDS, the body is weak and can't fight off infections, viruses and germs. HIV is the virus that is passed from one person to another. AIDS is the last stage of the illness.

5. **Could people tell by looking at Robert that he had HIV?**

    No. He looked and felt healthy at the time of the story.

6. **Any ideas of what HIV will do to Robert?**

Robert will probably look and feel healthy for a number of years. He may get some symptoms like swollen glands, fever or diarrhea. Then, because his immune system is weak, he may get a sickness like a rare cancer or pneumonia. He can die from one of these more serious sicknesses.

7. **How does a person get HIV?**

There are only a few ways that people get HIV. Sex without a condom is one way HIV is spread. Getting someone else's blood directly into your body is another way to get HIV. This can happen when people share needles (drug needles, tattoo or piercing needles). If a pregnant woman has HIV, her baby may be born with it. There is also a risk through breastfeeding when the mom has HIV.

8. **Robert says HIV is totally preventable. What does he mean?**

There are very good ways to prevent being infected with HIV. Using a condom can help stop the spread of HIV from one person to another. Using clean needles and not sharing the equipment to mix drugs is another way. People getting tattoos should always make sure that new needles, new ink and sterilized equipment are used. Pregnant women with HIV can take medication to keep from passing HIV to their unborn babies. A mother with HIV can feed her baby by bottle.

9. **While Robert was staying with Shay-Lyn and Tyler and their parents, it was okay to use the same cup as Robert. What two household items would they not want to share with him?**

The two items are a razor and a toothbrush, because they may have bits of blood on them.

10. **How long do you think Robert may live with HIV/AIDS?**

It depends on how well he looks after himself, and if he takes medication. Once HIV is in the body there is no way to get rid of it. People with HIV/AIDS will eventually die from it unless they die from something else first. Right now, some people live only a short time, but others live 10 years, 15, 20, 25 years or more. Scientists are doing research to find a cure, but until they succeed, medication helps people like Robert stay healthy longer. Robert can keep his immune system stronger if he eats well, continues his running and other exercise, and if he is not using drugs and alcohol.

11. **Can you think of some ways mentioned in the story that you cannot get HIV? Can I give you HIV by shaking your hand? Talking to you? Sneezing on you? By kissing? Being in a sweat lodge together? Sharing a drinking fountain, toys or clothes? What about from mosquitoes?**

No, you can't get HIV from any of these ways.

12. **What would you do if you came across someone who was bleeding?**

It is a good idea to get an adult to help you. Do not touch another person's blood. Since HIV is carried by blood, the adult would want to wear gloves while cleaning and bandaging the wound.

13. **What should you do if you find a needle somewhere? Who could you tell?**

Don't touch it! Find an adult like your teacher, a parent, a nurse, or a police officer. They would want to use tongs to pick it up and put it in a special "sharps" container (you may have seen one at the doctor's office) or a glass jar. They would also want to wear gloves.

14. **How do you think you would feel if other people called you names or were afraid of you because you knew someone with HIV or AIDS?**

Some people are not aware of how you get HIV and what is safe. Because they don't know about the virus, they are scared of someone with HIV. Talk to an adult you trust about your feelings. Shay-Lyn was puzzled and confused because Kelly couldn't play with her when Robert was visiting. Tyler was angry that people didn't understand.

15. **Who can you talk to if you have more questions about HIV?**

You can ask your teacher, a nurse, a doctor, a community health representative (CHR), your parents or guardians, or a health educator.

Questions written by Melanie Rivers, Educator, Chee Mamuk, Aboriginal program for culturally appropriate education about HIV/AIDS and STDs (sexually transmitted diseases). Reviewed by the STD Division, BC Centre for Disease Control. For more information and resources for teachers and adults on HIV/AIDS, go to Chee Mamuk's website at www.bccdc.org.

About Chee Mamuk

The Gathering Tree was initiated, supported and guided by Chee Mamuk, Aboriginal HIV/STI education program of the Division of STD/AIDS Control, British Columbia Centre for Disease Control (BCCDC), an agency of the Provincial Health Services Authority. Funding for the book was received from Provincial Health Services Authority, Aboriginal Health Initiatives.

Chee Mamuk is a provincial program, launched in 1989. Its mandate is to provide culturally appropriate on-site community-based HIV/AIDS and sexually transmitted infection education and training to Aboriginal communities, organizations and professionals within British Columbia.

Lucy Barney RN, MScN is the Chee Mamuk program manager. She is from the Stl'atl'imx Nation and incorporates her traditional knowledge into her current work.

Melanie Rivers BA is the Chee Mamuk educator. She is from the Squamish Nation and works with a holistic and community-based approach toward HIV/AIDS prevention and education.

Acknowledgements

Advisory Board for *The Gathering Tree*

Meg Hickling C.M., O.B.C. (North Vancouver), author and sexual health educator
Peter Jackson (Prince Rupert), sexual health educator specializing in First Nations youth and men's issues
Kate Kelsey RN (Vancouver), Nurse Educator, Street Nurse Program, STD/AIDS Control, BC Centre for Disease Control
Kecia Larkin (Victoria), APHA (Aboriginal Person Living with HIV/AIDS), Blackfoot and Kwa'kwa'ka'wakw Nations
Laura Rudland (Vancouver), Aboriginal Education Curriculum Consultant, Vancouver School District
Simone Shinder (Toronto), Director, Counseling Services, The Teresa Group, HIV Children's Counseling Service
Jane Wilde (Prince Rupert), sexual and reproductive health educator and nurse

Student Focus Groups

Admiral Seymour Elementary School, Vancouver, British Columbia
  Children and teachers of grades 6-7
  Rick Logie, Principal
  Donna Lokhorst, First Nations School Support Worker

Stein Valley Nlakapamux School, Lytton, British Columbia
  Children and teachers of grades 6-7
  Carol F. Michel, Principal

BC Centre for Disease Control

Michael Rekart MD, DTM & H Director, STD/AIDS Control
Gina Ogilvie MD, MSc Associate Director, STD/AIDS Control
Linda Knowles RN, BScN Clinic Nursing Administrator, STD/AIDS Control
Sally Greenwood BA Director, Communications, BC Centre for Disease Control and BC Transplant
Janine Stevenson, RN Registered Nurse, Street Nurse Program, STD/AIDS Control

Others

Theytus Books Ltd., Aboriginal Book Publisher, Penticton, British Columbia, Canada
Eleanor Kelly (Vancouver), mother of a PWA (person with AIDS) and AIDS Vancouver volunteer
tawx'sin yexwulla, Aaron Nelson Moody, Squamish Cultural Teacher
Temera Williams, Stl'atl'imx/Squamish, Teacher
Shayna Hornstein (Vancouver), long-time supporter of Chee Mamuk

For Further Information

Chee Mamuk, Aboriginal Program
STD/AIDS Control, BC Centre for Disease Control
655 W 12th Avenue
Vancouver, British Columbia
Canada V5Z 4R4
Tel: (604) 660-1673; Fax: (604) 775-0808

See www.bccdc.org, the Chee Mamuk website, for information for teachers and parents on HIV/AIDS resources.

The Gathering Tree

A children's book about HIV with a First Nations storyline

Includes study material for students, teachers, parents, health educators and others

The Gathering Tree is the gentle, positive story of a family facing HIV, told in a rural First Nations setting. After the children, 11-year-old Tyler and younger sister Shay-Lyn, learn their favorite cousin Robert has HIV, they discover that illness brings understanding and awareness. The children share a love of sports with Robert who has left their small community to go to school in the city. Robert is returning for a visit to attend the annual traditional community gathering. Kelly, Shay-Lyn's best friend, announces that she is not allowed to play with Shay-Lyn while Robert visits. Confused, the children ask their parents about Robert. They learn that he has HIV, and are anxious about his health. Will Robert die?

Robert arrives on the bus. The children are surprised to see he looks the same as ever. The family visits three elders at the river where Robert shares his feelings about being HIV positive. Tyler catches his first fish in the traditional way and a special ceremony is held in his honor. The children are given tobacco to burn in the fire as an offering so that all young people will keep safe and healthy.

Taking strength from the land, Robert is determined to run the annual marathon. Tyler wants to run the marathon with him. Because he is too young, Robert suggests he join the runners just before they arrive at the gathering. While he waits for Robert, Tyler finds strength and wisdom in the presence of the ancient tree watching over their people.

Encouraged by the elders, Robert talks to the gathering about his situation. Shay-Lyn and Tyler join Robert and elder Bill in an honor dance. Kelly joins them, showing that understanding is possible.

The story provides insights into ways of learning, the influence of elders in the community, and cultural activities such as traditional gatherings. Aspects of physical, spiritual, mental and emotional health are addressed.

Award-winning artist and illustrator Heather D. Holmlund's beautiful acrylic paintings bring the characters and rural setting to life.

The Authors and Illustrator

Author Larry Loyie was born in Slave Lake, Alberta. He spent his early years living a traditional Cree life and treasures the lessons he learned from the elders. He went to residential school from the age of 10 to 14, then began his working life. Larry returned to school later in life to fulfill his childhood dream of becoming a writer. He received the 2001 Canada Post Literacy Award for Individual Achievement (British Columbia). In 2003, Larry was the first First Nations writer to win the Norma Fleck Award for Canadian Children's Non-Fiction for his first children's book *As Long as the Rivers Flow*.

Co-author Constance Brissenden BA, MA is a freelance writer and editor. She is the author of 14 books of travel and history. In 1993, Constance and Larry formed Living Traditions Writers Group (www.firstnationswriter.com) to encourage First Nations people to write about their traditions and stories.

Illustrator Heather D. Holmlund has roots in the northern town of Fort Frances, Ontario, where she grew up. Her source of artistic vision has always been the spiritual essence of the Canadian landscape and its people. Heather attended York University in the visual arts program, before making her home in Pickering, Ontario. She is the award-winning illustrator of *As Long as the Rivers Flow*.